NICE NEW NEIGHBORS

FRANZ BRANDENBERG

illustrated by ALIKI

MULBERRY BOOKS • New York

Library of Congress Cataloging
in Publication Data
Brandenberg, Franz. Nice new neighbors.
(Greenwillow read-alone)
Summary: The Fieldmouse children find a way to
make new friends when they move to a new house.
[1. Friendship–Fiction. 2. Mice–Fiction]
I. Aliki. II. Title. PZ7.B7364Ni [E]
77-1651 ISBN 0-688-10997-7

for our nice old neighbor-friends
Hawley and Price

Come out
come out
wherever
you are

CONTENTS

CHAPTER 1

"Now that we have moved
into a nice new old house,
I hope you will make
nice new friends,"
said Mother Fieldmouse
to her six children.

"We will," said Annette,
Bertrand, Colette, Daniel,
Esther and Ferdinand.
"There is a nice family
living next door,"
said Father Fieldmouse.
"Their child is playing
jump rope."

"Jump rope is my favorite game,"
said Ferdinand.
"I am sure she'll let you
play with her,"
said Father Fieldmouse.
The Fieldmouse children
ran next door.

"May we play jump rope with you?"
asked Ferdinand.
"I don't need you,"
replied the neighbors' child.
"I like to play alone."

9

The Fieldmouse children
ran back home.
"The child next door won't let us
play with her," they cried.
"She will some day
when she knows you better,"
said Mother Fieldmouse.

"There is a nice family
living across the street,"
said Father Fieldmouse.
"Their children are playing tag."

"Tag is my favorite game,"
said Esther.
"I am sure they'll let you
play with them,"
said Father Fieldmouse.
The Fieldmouse children
ran across the street.

"May we play tag with you?"
asked Esther.

yoohoo

"We don't need you,"
replied the neighbors' children.
"There are enough of us."

13

The Fieldmouse children
ran back home.
"The children across the street
won't let us play with them,"
they cried.
"They will some day
when they know you better,"
said Mother Fieldmouse.

14

"There is a nice family
living up the street,"
said Father Fieldmouse.
"Their children are playing
ring-around-a-rosy."

"Ring-around-a-rosy is my
favorite game," said Daniel.
"I am sure they'll let you
play with them,"
said Father Fieldmouse.
The Fieldmouse children
ran up the street.

I've never seen Daniel run so fast!

"May we play ring-around-a-rosy
with you?" asked Daniel.
"We don't need you,"
replied the neighbors' children.
"There are enough of us."

hi

Ring around a rosy....

The Fieldmouse children
ran back home.
"The children up the street
won't let us play with them,"
they cried.
"They will some day
when they know you better,"
said Mother Fieldmouse.

There are
enough of us—
BAH!

Talk
about
unfriendly

18

Look what I see!

"There is a nice family
living around the corner,"
said Father Fieldmouse.
"Their children are playing
hide-and-seek."

19

Did you say "Hide-and-seek"?

"Hide-and-seek is my
favorite game," said Colette.
"I am sure they'll let you
play with them,"
said Father Fieldmouse.
The Fieldmouse children
ran around the corner.

"May we play hide-and-seek
with you?" asked Colette.
"We don't need you,"
replied the neighbors' children.
"There are enough of us."

No peeking, Alicia.

21

The Fieldmouse children
ran back home.
"The children around the corner
won't let us play with them,"
they cried.
"They will some day
when they know you better,"
said Mother Fieldmouse.

"Meanwhile, why don't you play your own game?" said Father Fieldmouse. "There are enough of you."

23

CHAPTER 2

The Fieldmouse children
ran to their garage.
"Let's do a play!"
said Annette.
"Hurrah!" shouted Bertrand.

24

"That's even better than playing hide-and-seek," said Colette.

"That's even better than playing ring-around-a-rosy," said Daniel.

"That's even better than playing tag," said Esther.

"That's even better than playing jump rope," said Ferdinand.

"What is the play called?" asked Bertrand.

" 'Three Blind Mice!' " replied Annette.

"How does it go?" asked Colette.

"It goes like this," said Annette.

"Three blind mice!
Three blind mice!
See how they run!
See how they run!
They all ran after
the farmer's wife.
She cut off their tails
with a carving knife.
Did you ever see
such a sight in your life
As three blind mice?"

"That's very nice,"
they all said.

very

nice

27

"What part am I going to play?"
asked Bertrand.

"You, Colette and Daniel will play
the blind mice," said Annette.

"I will play the farmer's wife."

WOW!
The stars!

what about us?

28

"We'd like a part, too,"

said Esther and Ferdinand.

"There are no more parts,"

said Annette.

"We could always make

some up," said Bertrand.

"All right," said Annette.

"You can be the parents."

yes, children.
No ice cream for
bad tempers!

Waa
Waa

29

"May we have a part, too?"
asked the children
from across the street.
"We don't need you,"
replied Annette.
"There are enough of us."

"Besides, there are no parts for lizards," said Bertrand.

"We could always make some up," said Esther.

"All right," said Annette. "You can be the police."

"May I have a part, too?"

asked the child from next door.

"We don't need you," replied Annette.

"There are enough of us."

"Besides, there is no part

for a frog," said Bertrand.

"We could always make one up,"

said Ferdinand.

"All right," said Annette.

"You can be the judge."

me?
a judge?

33

"May we have a part, too?"

asked the children

from around the corner.

"We don't need you," replied Annette.

"There are enough of us."

"Besides, there are no parts

for snails," said Bertrand.

"We could always make some up,"

said Colette.

"All right," said Annette.

"You can be witnesses."

Vasilios. What's yours.

I've never been a judge before.

the more the merrier

35

"May we have a part, too?"

asked the children

from up the street.

"We don't need you,"

replied Annette.

"There are enough of us."

It's getting crowded.

Don't make fun, Bertrand!

"Besides, there are no parts
for grasshoppers," said Bertrand.
"We could always make some up,"
said Daniel.
"All right," said Annette.
"You can be tailors."

37

NEIGHBORHOOD
PRODUCTIONS
PRESENTS:

THREE
BLIND
MICE

My, they're so organized!

Come on, Tillie. Do we always have to be last?

We're Helen's parents.

I would have recognized you anywhere!

38

CHAPTER 3

The children rehearsed
the play all day.
In the evening,
the whole neighborhood
came to see it.

39

Act 1

Three blind mice! Three blind mice!

After her, men.

Look what I see.

See how they run! See how they run!

I'll fix them.

This way, Daniel!

They all ran after the farmer's wife.

40

She cut off their tails with a carving knife.

Did you ever see such a sight in your life

As three blind mice?

41

The mice ran to their parents.

The parents ran to the police.

The police ran after the farmer's wife.

42

They took her to court with her carving knife.

The judge told the court at once to begin.

He asked the witnesses what they had seen.

43

The witnesses swore

that the farmer's wife

had cut off the tails with a carving knife.

immediately

My what!

The judge then ordered the farmer's wife

alas — my collection.

to give up the tails and the carving knife.

Easy does it.

Hold still, now.

Three tailors sewed the tails back on.

Never, never again.

The farmer's wife begged,

"Forgive what I've done!"

Please

me ?

She invited the parents, the judge,

follow me

the police, the tailors and the witnesses,

46

and, of course, the three blind mice,

homemade, naturally

to her farm, for blueberry ice.

Did she say homemade?

They all ran after the farmer's wife.

Did she say blueberry?

Did you ever see such a sight in your life?

The audience applauded wildly.
They had never seen
such a sight in their lives.
"Aren't we lucky to have
such nice new neighbors!"
they all said.

hi, ma

shh

BRAVO

I didn't know they could sew!

AUTHOR!

ENCORE!!

Maybe there's an opening on Broadway...

A born actress.

I could cry.

CHAPTER 4

The next day,
the Fieldmouse children played
with the Frog child,
the Lizard children,
the Grasshopper children,
and the Snail children.

They played hide-and-seek,

Yoohoo over here!

Here I come — ready or not!

We'll sit this one out.

Can't catch a butterfly

Come on, Annette!

They could Qualify for the Olympics!

tag,

whee

Look at her go!

Shall we try?

jump rope,

Ring around a rosy

and ring-around-a-rosy.

pocKet full of posy

"We are glad you made

such nice new friends,"

said Mother and Father Fieldmouse.

"We said we would,"

said the Fieldmouse children.